2/04

D0042201

Buried Treasure

ALL ABOUT USING A MAP

Written by Kirsten Hall

Illustrated by Bev Luedecke

children's press®

A Division of Scholastic Inc.
New York Toronto London Auckland Sydney
Mexico City New Delhi Hong Kong
Danbury, Connecticut

About the Author

Kirsten Hall, formerly an early-childhood teacher,
is a children's book editor in New York City. She has been
writing books for children since she was thirteen years old
and now has over sixty titles in print.

About the Illustrator

Bev Luedecke enjoys life and nature in Colorado.
Her sparkling personality and artistic flair are reflected in her
creation of Beastieville, a world filled with lovable Beasties
sure to delight children of all ages.

Library of Congress Cataloging-in-Publication Data

Hall, Kirsten.
  Buried treasure : all about using a map / written by Kirsten Hall ;
illustrated by Bev Luedecke.
      p. cm.
Summary: Flippet finds a map that appears to lead to buried treasure,
but her friends discover a treasure that is "berried" instead.
  ISBN 0-516-22894-3 (lib. bdg.)   0-516-24652-6 (pbk.)
  [1. Buried treasure–Fiction. 2. Maps–Fiction. 3. Berries–Fiction. 4.
Stories in rhyme.] I. Luedecke, Bev, ill. II. Title.
  PZ8.3.H146Bv 2003
  [E]–dc21
                                        2003001588

1 2 3 4 5 6 7 8 9 10 R 12 11 10 09 08 07 06 05 04 03

A NOTE TO PARENTS AND TEACHERS

Welcome to the world of the Beasties, where learning is FUN. In each of the charming stories in this series, the Beasties deal with character issues that every child can identify with. Each story reinforces appropriate concept skills for kindergartners and first graders, while simultaneously encouraging problem-solving skills. Following are just a few of the ways in which you can help children get the most from this delightful series.

Stories to be read and enjoyed

Encourage children to read the stories aloud. The rhyming verses make them fun to read. Then ask them to think about alternate solutions to some of the problems that the Beasties have faced or to imagine alternative endings. Invite children to think about what they would have done if they were in the story and to recall similar things that have happened to them.

Activities reinforce the learning experience

The activities at the end of the books offer a way for children to put their new skills to work. They complement the story and are designed to help children develop specific skills and build confidence. Use these activities to reinforce skills. But don't stop there. Encourage children to find ways to build on these skills during the course of the day.

Learning opportunities are everywhere

Use this book as a starting point for talking about how we use reading skills or math or social studies concepts in everyday life. When we search for a phone number in the telephone book and scan names in alphabetical order or check a list, we are using reading skills. When we keep score at a baseball game or divide a class into even-numbered teams, we are using math.

The more you can help children see that the skills they are learning in school really do have a place in everyday life, the more they will think of learning as something that is part of their lives, not as a chore to be borne. Plus you will be sending the important message that learning is fun.

Madeline Boskey Olsen, Ph.D.
Developmental Psychologist

Bee-Bop

Puddles

Slider

Wilbur

Pip & Zip

Flippet

Pooky

Mr. Rigby

We're
the
Beasties

Smudge

Toggles

What a lovely sunny day!
Flippet swims beneath a tree.
There is something in the mud.
She wonders, "What is that I see?"

Flippet rushes over to it.
"What is this? What have I found?
It looks like a treasure map!
Who has left it on the ground?"

"I must find my friends to show them!
They will want to see this, too!
Should I try to find the treasure?
Someone must know what to do!"

10

She finds Slider in his yard.
"Slider! Come and look at this!
Might this be a treasure map?"
Slider gives a nod and hiss.

"This map leads to buried treasure!
We must go get Zip and Pip.

They are very good with numbers.
They can help us on our trip!"

"Now we are outside the schoolhouse.
On the map we start right here.

First we must pass four blue houses.
Then turn left. We must be near!"

"Mr. Rigby, come and join us!
Toggles, come and join us, too!
We will find some buried treasure!
Bee-Bop, tell us what to do!"

"First we must pass six red flowers.
Now we turn left at the store.

We must pass four rocks and turn right.
I see the house with the red door!"

"Oh, we must be very close now!
Stop before that big oak tree.

Take a left, now take a right.
Look at that! What could it be?"

"Look at all those Beastie berries!
Maybe we should stop to eat!

Have you ever seen such berries?
I would bet that these are sweet!"

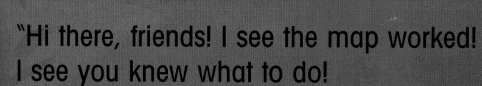

"Hi there, friends! I see the map worked!
I see you knew what to do!

You thought it was buried treasure?
I guess these are treasures, too!"

"Pooky! Yes, you really tricked us!
Berry treasures! You are right!
First we can have some to eat.
Then we can have a berry fight."

TREASURE COUNT

1. How many green stripes does Slider have?

2. How many purple stripes does Slider have?

3. How many orange stripes does Slider have?

4. How many stripes does Slider have in all?

SOUNDS LIKE...

The word "flap"
sounds a lot like "map".
Can you think of other words
that sound like "map"?

LET'S TALK ABOUT IT

Flippet and Slider did not keep the treasure map a secret from the other Beasties.

1. Why do you think they wanted to tell their friends about the map?

2. Why might they have kept it a secret?

3. Pooky had a very clever way of surprising her friends. Have you ever surprised someone else by doing something that was really nice?

WORD LIST

a	Flippet	like	schoolhouse	thought
all	flowers	look	see	to
and	found	looks	seen	Toggles
are	four	lovely	she	too
at	friends	map	should	treasure
be	get	maybe	show	treasures
Beastie	gives	might	six	tree
Bee-Bop	go	Mr. Rigby	Slider	tricked
before	good	mud	some	trip
beneath	ground	must	someone	try
berries	guess	my	something	turn
berry	has	near	start	us
bet	have	nod	stop	very
big	help	now	store	want
blue	here	numbers	such	was
buried	hi	oak	summer	we
can	his	oh	sweet	what
close	hiss	on	swims	who
come	house	our	take	will
could	houses	outside	tell	with
day	I	over	that	wonders
do	in	pass	the	worked
door	is	Pip	them	would
eat	it	Pooky	then	yard
ever	join	really	there	yes
fight	knew	red	these	you
find	know	right	they	Zip
finds	leads	rocks	this	
first	left	rushes	those	